THIS CANDLEWICK BOOK BELONGS TO:

_____

_____

_____

Not so long ago, a tooth fairy
took a call on her cell phone.
"April Underhill here."
With one finger in her ear to block
the traffic noise, she listened.
"You're his grandma?
No, my sister, Esme, and I
don't do tooth visits yet.
Our mom and dad always . . .
You want US?
We shall be there.
I PROMISE."

For Lola, Sadie, and Poppy

First U.S. paperback edition 2013

The Library of Congress has cataloged the hardcover edition as follows:

Graham, Bob, date.
 April and Esme, tooth fairies / Bob Graham. — 1st U.S. ed.
    p. cm.
 Summary: On their first assignment, two young tooth fairy sisters journey by night into the huge world of
humans to collect Daniel Dangerfield's tooth and fly it safely home.
 ISBN 978-0-7636-4683-7 (hardcover)
 ISBN 978-0-7636-6347-6 (paperback)
 [1. Tooth Fairy—Fiction. 2. Fairies—Fiction. 3. Sisters—Fiction.] I. Title.
 PZ7.G751667Ap 2010
 [E]—dc22   2009049082

CCP 18 17 16 15 14 13
10 9 8 7 6 5 4 3 2 1

Printed in Shenzhen, Guangdong, China

This book was typeset in Poliphilus and Blado MT.
The illustrations were done in ink and watercolor.

Candlewick Press
99 Dover Street
Somerville, Massachusetts 02144

visit us at www.candlewick.com

April and Esme
Tooth Fairies

Bob Graham

The North
M 42

CANDLEWICK PRESS

April Underhill opened the door.
A draft slipped through behind her and Esme,
making the teeth hanging from the rafters chatter and chime.
John Underhill started to speak. "April . . ."

"Don't say anything, Daddy,"
April said. "We're collecting
a boy's tooth tonight, and
I have to write this down. . . ."

Daniel
Dangerfield
3 Cornflower
Terrace
Parkville Milk
Tooth front
Dog. no Cat
Tonihgt

"*Tonight?* April, you're
only seven," said her dad.
"And three quarters," April
added. "I promised."

"I'm going too,"
said Esme.

"You and Esme? A tooth in Parkville?" said their mom, Fay.
"Darlings, you're far too young."

"You went by yourself when you were six, Mommy," said Esme.
  She balanced a bubble on the end of her finger till it popped.
"Same age as me—and April's even older."

"Well, that was long ago," said Mom. "Before the highway came.

Foxes still chased hares on the hill, and things were different back then."

"Well, some things haven't changed, Mommy."
Esme took a sip of her dandelion soup.
"Children still lose their first teeth," April said,
"and ducklings still have to take their first swim."

Their parents looked at them, startled.
"OK," said Dad. "You can both go—but
take great care of your little sister, April."

"Yes!"

"This is important, April," said Dad.
"To Daniel you are a . . . a . . . spirit of the air.
You are magic. He must never see you."

"Magic? *Me?*" said April.

Mom found a string bag.
"For the coin going out—and
the tooth coming back," she said.

"Send me a text if you need to," she added.

Then
they
lifted off
into the night.

The North
M42 ↑

and shook them . . .

pushed them and pulled them.

The wind took them . . .   It shivered down Esme's wings . . .

and rippled through the feathers of a passing owl.

"There's Cornflower Terrace!" shouted April.

They dropped through the dark . . .

right onto the doorstep of Daniel's house.
They peered underneath.

April swallowed. "Hold down my wings, Esme. I'll go first."

Esme crawled in after her . . .

to the other side. "Where is his room?" she whispered.

"Up there, I think," replied April.
"Let's follow the toys."

"This must be him," whispered April.
She pulled the note from her pocket.
"We're at Three Cornflower Terrace,"
she said. "There's a dog, but no cat—"
"And THERE'S THE TOOTH!"
cried Esme, shivering with excitement.

"But, oh dear!
He's put it in water,"
said April.

She made a decision. "I can swim. I'll get it."

She squeezed her eyes shut and,
in a cloud of bubbles, went for the bottom.
"I've got it, Esme! I've got it!"

"Shhh!" hissed Esme . . .

as Daniel Dangerfield stirred . . .

and woke up!

April flew and Esme followed her. Together they
pulled Daniel's eyes shut, like blinds over windows.
For a long time, they didn't dare to breathe.

"He's asleep again," April whispered.
"But he *saw* us," Esme whispered back.

"I'll text Mommy,"
said April.

"Whisper what?"
Esme asked as
they read her reply.

"What Daddy told us.
That we're spirits."

"You do it, April,"
said Esme.
"Me? I'm soaked."

But she leaned into the dark and whispered,
"We're spirits of the air, Daniel. You dreamed us.
You did not see us."

"April, wait!" called Esme.

"It's the sweetest sight. . . .

"Good-bye, Daniel Dangerfield!"
They picked up the tooth and
flew down the hall.

I think it's the grandma."

April waded waist-deep in Grandma's hair, then kissed her on the nose. "We did it, Grandma. Our very first tooth," she whispered. "No, Esme, we don't take those. We have to go."

They collected their coats,
buttoned them tight,
and slipped
under the door.

Daniel's front tooth swung
in its bag as they cleared
the chimney and headed
for home.

The wind tumbled them
high over the city,
up the highway,
and set them down . . .

at their own front door.
Mom and Dad hugged
them till their wings
crackled.

"Here's the tooth, Daddy,
    wrapped in my wet undershirt."
"You dived for it?" asked Fay.

"Like a duckling in water,"
    murmured John Underhill
proudly.

The girls drank hot elderberry juice
and then were hugged some more.

Mom hung Daniel's tooth from the rafters.
"On Saturday, we'll take it to the Fairy Craft Market
for everyone to see," Dad promised.

The sun rose, and a blackbird sang outside the window,
louder than the distant traffic. As April and Esme fell asleep . . .

Daniel Dangerfield woke to find a coin gleaming by his bedside.
A new tooth was already coming in. What dreams he'd had!

Out on the highway,
a wild hare scampered across
six lanes of traffic,
    past an old stump,
        a tiny house,
and up to its time-worn
tracks on the hill.
Nose twitching, it looked over
its shoulder for foxes,
then far out to the horizon. . . .

Bob Graham is the author-illustrator of many acclaimed books for children, including *How to Heal a Broken Wing*, which won the Charlotte Zolotow Award and about which *Booklist* said in a starred review, "This is such a visual piece . . . readers, young and old, will return to the story to look more deeply; they won't be disappointed." His other titles include *A Bus Called Heaven*, *"Let's Get a Pup!" Said Kate*, *"The Trouble with Dogs . . ." Said Dad*, and *Dimity Dumpty*. He also illustrated *I'm Number One*, written by Michael Rosen. Bob Graham lives in Australia.